Max Beerbohm

Caricatures of twenty-five gentlemen

Max Beerbohm

Caricatures of twenty-five gentlemen

ISBN/EAN: 9783741191619

Manufactured in Europe, USA, Canada, Australia, Japa

Cover: Foto ©Andreas Hilbeck / pixelio.de

Manufactured and distributed by brebook publishing software
(www.brebook.com)

Max Beerbohm

Caricatures of twenty-five gentlemen

MR. HALL CAINE.
(A CARICATURE BY MAX BEERBOHM.)

CARICATURES

OF

TWENTY-FIVE GENTLEMEN

BY

MAX BEERBOHM

CARICATURES

OF

TWENTY-FIVE GENTLEMEN

BY

MAX BEERBOHM

WITH AN INTRODUCTION BY L. RAVEN-HILL

LEONARD SMITHERS

4 AND 5 ROYAL ARCADE: OLD BOND STREET

LONDON W

1896

PREFACE

WE have working among us some score of artists who produce humorous drawings week by week, and to whom the term "caricaturist" is loosely applied. As a matter of fact, we—for even I have been so honoured—do not caricature at all. We take a notion that appears to us interesting, and work it up with various accessories into a more or less humorous drawing. We do not necessarily *exaggerate*: we *reproduce* the incongruities of life.

There is another kind of humourist who is inaccurately called a caricaturist. He concerns himself chiefly with the persons of our prominent statesmen, and his drawings are political rather than personal skits—his first business being with the political position rather than the personal appearance of his victims. Of course he does caricature to a certain extent. He gets a certain formula—an eyeglass or a double chin or an umbrella—to express the personality of his subject in a more or less ridiculous manner, and that is sufficient. He does not intentionally ridicule *the whole man*, but one or two of his characteristics. What he aims at is to present a political allegory. So he turns his man into a cock crowing in a farmyard, or a nurse with a baby, or whatever strikes him as appropriate at the moment. His caricaturing is perfunctory, and I have noticed that, when he draws for a Radical paper, he is apt to idealise Sir William Harcourt.

There are others who do so-called "caricatures" of politicians in the Lobby, or of actors and actresses in a new play. These are nearer to being caricaturists, for they aim at ridiculing personal appearances apart from anything else. But their work is seldom real caricature. Possibly they are too good-natured. They exaggerate one or two points and leave the rest approximately correct.

Now Max *is* a caricaturist. For him Man exists only to be caricatured and his possibilities revealed, no part of him, from his head to his heel, being more worthy of ridicule than another. If Max sees a little man with nothing particularly strange about him except a big moustache, he goes for that big moustache, it becomes bigger and bigger, until it overwhelms everything else. Everything dwindles beside it, getting smaller and smaller in the right proportion.

People have often said of Max, "Oh, but he can't draw." I know he can't correctly reproduce a foot or the shadows on a face, and that his perspective is apt to be a bit primitive; but he makes up greatly for this lack of technical knowledge by a charming freedom of line. There is no stiffness in his drawings, and some of them are distinctly decorative. Pellegrini (the unforgettable "Ape") knew how to draw, and the limbs or features of his subjects, however much he distorted them, were always real limbs or features. Max often takes refuge in a sort of symbolism, in order to avoid difficulties of draughtsmanship. On the whole, I would not advise him to *learn* drawing seriously—the process would probably cramp him and take from him much of that delightful irreverence for things as they are, which is really one of his strongest points.

As it is, Max never draws from the life. I don't know that people would consent to sit to him if he wanted them to. When he meets anyone he wishes to immortalise, he looks his victim full in the face—a habit which is often taken to denote his frank and honest nature, until his reason is known. The impression of his subject thus sinks into his mind, and when he sits down to draw, the *salient* features stand out in his memory, while the rest are to a great extent ignored. Since "Ape" there has been no one with such an awful instinct for the principal parts of a man's appearance. Look at each of these caricatures, and see how one or two things in each are elaborated and magnified, and how slightly he deals with the rest. His instinct for style and character is wonderful. He gives you a savage epitome of a man's exterior, and, through that, the quintessence of the man himself. He is a psychologist in drawing if ever there was one.

It is a mistake to suppose that everybody can understand and enjoy caricatures more easily than any other sort of art. When I was assisting in the management of a periodical to which Max was contributing a series of caricatures, we used to get letters from people all over the country, pointing out that Mr. Blank was not half so fat, or Lord Dash not half so bald as Max had made him, or Mr. Blank-Dash hadn't got legs like pins. Max's caricatures are difficult to the public at large, partly because the public is not accustomed to seeing real caricatures, and partly because, in many cases, it is not well acquainted with the person caricatured. I do not know if Max knows his people well, but I have invariably found that a caricature of his that has not greatly struck me at first, has always become marvellous in resemblance as I have known the subject of it better.

I am extremely glad to have had the opportunity of expressing my admiration for Max's work. I do not think it can be discussed by any rule of three argument such as might be applied to more academic or matter of fact productions. One either likes it immensely or does not like it at all, and I hope that a considerable portion of the people who see this book will be amongst those who do.

L. RAVEN-HILL.

CONTENTS

TO THE SHADE
OF
CARLO PELLEGRINI

THE RIGHT HON. THE EARL OF ROSEBERY, K.G.

MR. ARTHUR WING PINERO.

HIS ROYAL HIGHNESS THE PRINCE OF WALES, K.G.

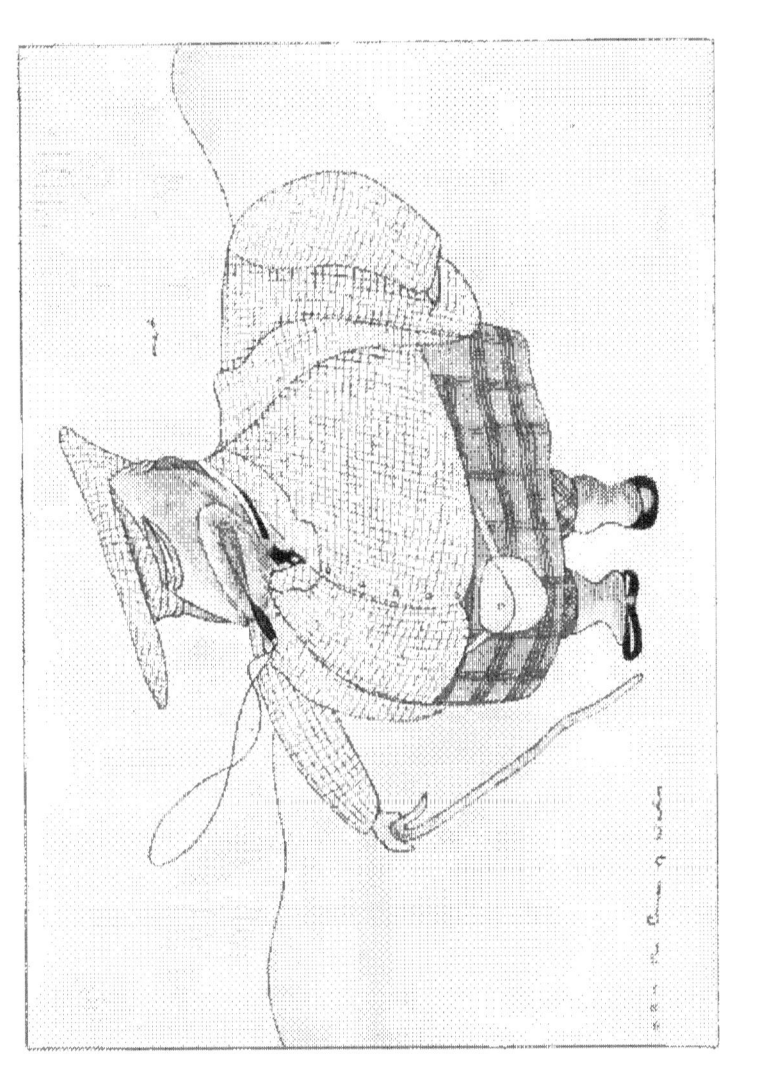

RICHARD·LE·GALLIENNE   MAX

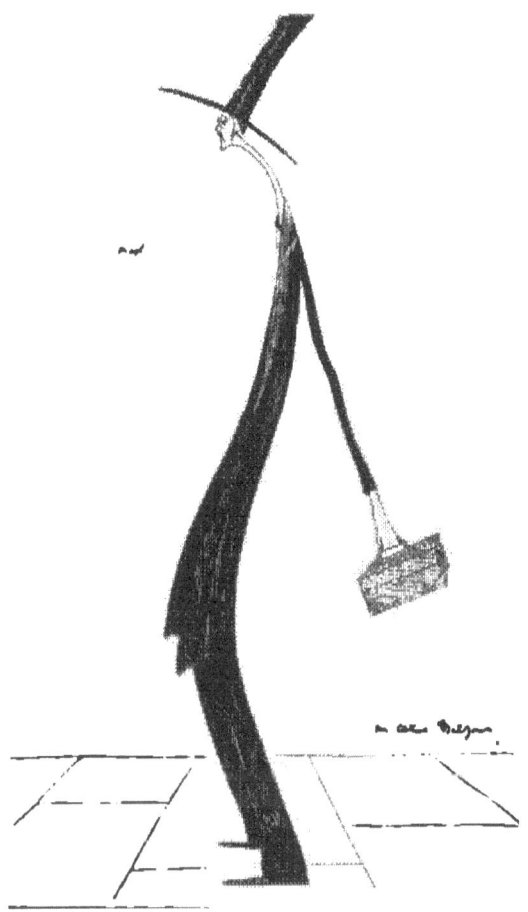

MR. FRANK HARRIS.

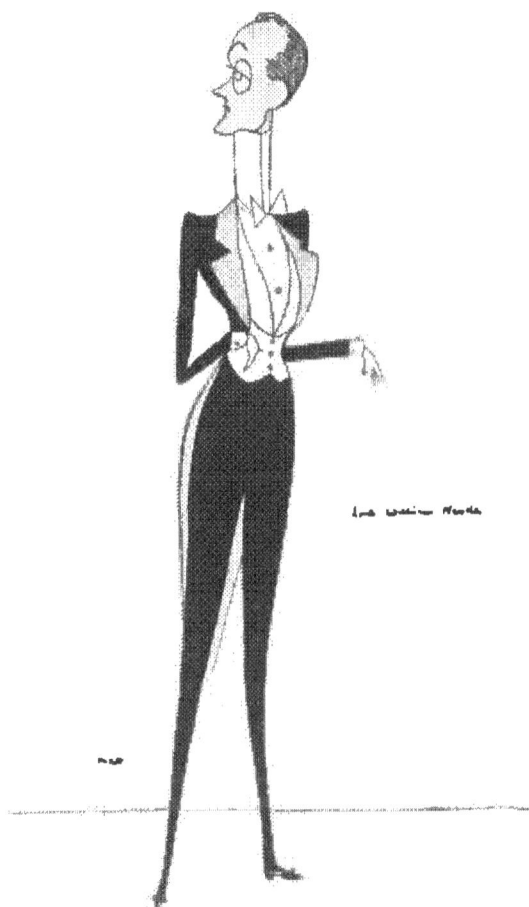

Mr. Rudyard Kipling

THE RIGHT HON. SIR WILLIAM VERNON V. HARCOURT, M.P.

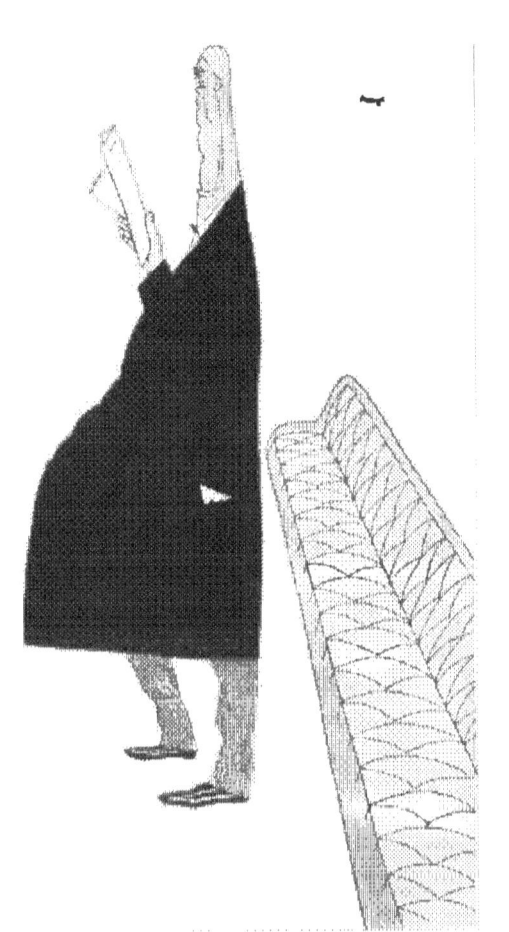

Max

The Warden
of Merton

JOSEPH CHAMBERLAIN

MAX

MR. GEORGE BERNARD SHAW.

George Bernard Shaw Esq

Sir George Lewis

H.R.H. The Duke of Cambridge

MR. GEORGE MOORE.

LORD GEORGE   MAX

LORD GRANBY   MAX

MR. HERBERT BEERBOHM TREE.